Get-Better
Jelly

Look out for more

Bake a Wish

books:

Feel Good Fairy Cakes

Can-Do Crispies

Feel Fearless Flapjacks

Bake a Wish

Get-Better Jelly

Lorna Honeywell

Illustrated by Samantha Chaffey

■SCHOLASTIC

With special thanks to Sue Mongredien

First published in the UK in 2012 by Scholastic Children's Books
An imprint of Scholastic Ltd
Euston House, 24 Eversholt Street
London, NW1 1DB, UK
Registered office: Westfield Road, Southam, Warwickshire, CV47 0RA
SCHOLASTIC and associated logos are trademarks and/or
registered trademarks of Scholastic Inc.

Text copyright © Hothouse Fiction Limited, 2012
Illustrations copyright © Samantha Chaffey, 2012

The right of Lorna Honeywell and Samantha Chaffey to be identified as the
author and illustrator of this work has been asserted by them.
Produced by Hothouse Fiction.
www.hothousefiction.com

Cover illustration © Katie May Green, 2012

ISBN 978 1 407 13115 3

A CIP catalogue record for this book is available from the British Library.

Printed and bound by CPI Group (UK) Ltd, Croydon, CR0 4YY
Papers used by Scholastic Children's Books are made from
wood grown in sustainable forests.

1 3 5 7 9 10 8 6 4 2

www.scholastic.co.uk/zone

For Holly Powell, who is an ace baker.

And for Auriol Bussell,

the best grandma anyone could wish for.

Where's Grandma?

Lily Dalton ran into the sunny playground
with her best friend, Antonia. "I'm a
giant," she giggled, taking huge stretchy
strides across the playground. "Can you
feel the ground shaking?"

"Oh yes!" Antonia laughed, stomping
fiercely. Lily laughed too. She and Antonia
had just had a really fun drama class
where the teacher had asked everyone to
walk in all sorts of different ways.

They'd scuttled like crabs, fluttered like

fairies and hopped like baby rabbits.
Lily had enjoyed being a giant best
of all, though, especially when she got
to practise a giant, booming voice
too!

Lily took long, stompy steps all the
way across the playground, imagining the
concrete cracking beneath her heavy giant
feet, and insects and animals running for
cover.

Lily clomped over to the willow tree
at the edge of the playground where her
grandma and her little brother Archie
usually waited for her after school. Lily
and Archie went back to Grandma and
Grandpa's house every day and stayed
there until Mum and Dad finished work
and came to pick them up. But today
Grandma and Archie weren't there –
Grandpa was instead!

Grandpa looked as if he'd come straight
from the garden because his brown
corduroy trousers were a bit muddy
on his knees, and he was wearing his
favourite gardening hat. "Hello, Lily," he

called, his blue eyes twinkling when he saw her.

"Hi, Grandpa," Lily said, hugging him. He smelled like peppermint and grass clippings as usual. "Where's Grandma? And where's Archie?"

"Archie's not feeling very well," Grandpa said. "He had to come home from his nursery school early, so Grandma's looking after him at home."

Lily felt sorry for her little brother. Being ill was horrible! On the way back to Grandma and Grandpa's house, she wondered if there was anything she could do to make Archie feel better. Maybe she would tell him an exciting story about dinosaurs, she thought to herself. Archie loved dinosaurs!

"Here we are," Grandpa said when they reached the house. "Do you want to help me check the strawberries in the vegetable patch? It's been so sunny lately, I have a feeling some of them might be ripe already."

Lily really loved strawberries. Just thinking about biting into the juicy red berries was enough to make her mouth water. But she knew what a good big sister should do. "I'd better go and say hello to Grandma and poor old Archie," she said. "But don't eat all the strawberries without me, Grandpa!"

Grandpa gave a rumbly laugh. "I'll save you one or two," he said. Then he put his finger to his lips. "Creep in quietly, won't you?" he added. "We don't want to disturb Archie if he's asleep."

Lily remembered her drama class where the teacher had asked them to tiptoe across the room as quietly as mice. She crept into the house on the very tips of her toes without making a sound. She imagined her mouse nose twitching, her mouse ears pricked up and her long, pink mouse tail swinging behind her. As she crept through the kitchen she spotted Hector, Grandma's marmalade-coloured cat, watching her sleepily from where he lay curled in a sunny spot. Just for a second, Lily forgot she wasn't really a mouse and nearly let out a squeak of fright!

"Oh, Hector," she giggled, stroking his soft ginger fur. "I'm glad I'm a girl, not a mouse. I wouldn't want you to pounce on me."

Hector purred contentedly, his green eyes closing again as he drifted back to sleep.

Lily gave him one last stroke and set off to find Grandma and Archie. As she went past the old wooden dresser, her heart beat a little faster at the sight of Grandma's special jar on the top shelf. Although it might *look* ordinary, Lily knew that it was full of magical surprises!

In the living room, Lily found Archie lying on Grandma's squishy red sofa with a blanket over him and his eyes shut. His cheeks were bright pink, and Grandma had her hand on his forehead like Lily's mum sometimes did to check their temperatures.

Grandma smiled when she saw Lily. "Hello, Lilybee," she whispered, tiptoeing towards her. "Let's go in the kitchen. He's just fallen asleep."

Back in the kitchen, Grandma poured Lily a glass of cold orange juice and washed a red apple for her. "Poor Archie's got a sore throat and a cough, and he's a bit hot," she said. "He says his head hurts too. I've given him some medicine and a nice cool drink, and I'm sure a little sleep will do him good."

"I wish I had a magic wand," Lily said. "I'd use it to magic Archie all better with my special fairy powers."

Grandma hugged her. "I wish you could magic him better too," she said. "But don't worry. Everyone gets poorly sometimes. It won't be long until he's back to his usual cheerful self!"

* * 8 *
* *

Just then, a sunbeam streamed through the kitchen window. The light fell on Grandma's white jar with yellow stripes, making it gleam and sparkle. And in that very moment, Lily had an idea. An idea so brilliant and perfect it  made her feel tingly all over. "I know, Grandma!" she cried. "We could look in the magic jar! Maybe there's a magical recipe inside that will make Archie better!"

2

Inside the Magic Jar

Grandma smiled. "That's a *very* good idea," she said.

Lily grinned as she thought about the magic jar. Whenever they needed it, a new recipe and some ingredients would magically appear inside it, and it would always be exactly the right thing to fix their problems.

The first time they'd used it, the jar had given them a recipe for Feel Good Fairy Cakes, which had been so delicious they'd got rid of a very bad case of the grumps. Last time, there had been a recipe for Can-Do Crispies, which had made Lily brave enough to perform in her Easter show.

What would the magic jar give them

this time? Lily was beginning to feel shivery with excitement. She couldn't wait to find out!

Grandma went over to the dresser and was just reaching up to get the magic jar when there was a cough from the other room.

"Grandma?" Archie called in a croaky voice.

"Why don't you go and say hello and see if Archie's OK?" Grandma asked Lily as she lifted the jar down. "He might need another drink."

Lily went in to see her brother. His face still looked red and hot but his eyes were open now. "Hi, Archie," she said softly, sitting down next to him. "Do you want some water?"

Archie nodded. Lily passed him his drink, and he slowly sat up and took a few sips. Then he flopped back down on the sofa cushion and shut his eyes again.

Lily stroked his hot head, smoothing back his wavy brown hair. "Me and Grandma are going to use a recipe from the magic jar to cook something to make you feel better," she whispered to him. "It'll be extra special, just like you!"

Archie's eyes stayed closed but his eyelids fluttered and his mouth twisted up in a little smile, as if he liked the sound of that.

Lily watched him as he fell asleep again. Hopefully he would have a lovely dream about Grandma's magic jar, she thought. Archie loved helping Grandma with her special recipes!

The magic jar was on the table when Lily went back into the kitchen. "Is Archie all right?" Grandma asked as she put on her favourite apron with bright red flowers and fastened it around her waist.

"He had another drink and now he's gone to sleep again," Lily replied. "He didn't seem very well at all. I'm glad we're making something to make him feel better." She went to get her own special apron, which hung from a hook on the back of the kitchen door. Since they'd started doing more cooking together, Grandma had bought Lily and

Archie their very
own aprons. Lily's
was yellow and
white, with pockets
shaped like cupcakes,
and Archie's was
covered with pictures
of all different types
of dinosaurs.

"Well, here's the
magic jar," Grandma
said, her eyes
twinkling behind her
spectacles as she smiled at Lily. "So when
you're ready, we'll make our wish."

Lily tied her apron strings around
her middle, just like Grandma, and
rushed over to the kitchen table. "I'm
ready," she said, her tummy feeling jumpy
with excitement.

Hector sat up very straight, blinked twice and gazed at Lily and Grandma with his green eyes wide. He even gave a little meow, as if to say, *Come on, then, hurry up. What's inside the jar today?*

Grandma laughed. "All right, Hector, be patient," she said. She put her hand on the lid of the jar and smiled at Lily. "Make a wish," she whispered.

Lily put her hand on the jar too. It was cool and smooth under her fingers and she felt a bit sad that Archie's hand wasn't there with hers today, as well. "I wish Archie wasn't poorly," she said, thinking of him lying in the other room, feeling hot and unwell. Then she blinked as something blue fluttered past the kitchen window. Was it a fairy, coming to magically make Archie better?

Lily gasped and rubbed her eyes. When

she looked again she saw that it was just
a big blue butterfly, dancing through the
sunny garden. Lily wasn't too disappointed,
though — she didn't need a fairy if she
had baking magic!

"That's a very good wish," Grandma
said. "I wish that Archie would start
feeling better too." She winked. "Well, let's
see what's inside it this time."

Lily took her hand off the jar as
Grandma lifted the lid. Lily peered eagerly
inside. There was a rolled-up piece of
paper and three packets of red jelly.

Lily dipped her hand in and took
everything out. The packets of jelly
gleamed like rubies when she put them
on the sunny table. "Strawberry flavour —
yum!" she smiled.

Then Grandma uncurled the paper.
"Oh good, the jar has done it again," she

said. "This is just what we need!"

"What is it, Grandma?" Lily gasped.

Grandma looked at her, her eyes twinkling. "It's a recipe for Get-Better Jelly!"

3

Get-Better Jelly!

Lily read out the ingredients for the
Get Better Jelly. "We need jelly cubes,
hot water, cold lemonade and fresh
strawberries," she said. "And it
says to use a jelly mould if
we have one. Do we have
one, Grandma?"

Grandma smiled. "We
certainly do," she said.
"In fact, there's a very
special jelly mould in

21 ★ ★
★

the cupboard with all the pots and pans.
It has long ears and a twitchy nose. . . I
wonder if you can guess what it is?"

Lily gaped. "A jelly mould with long
ears and a twitchy nose?" she echoed,
rushing over to the cupboard excitedly.
What could it be?

Grandma laughed. "Have a look inside.
I'm sure you'll find it," she said.

Lily opened the cupboard door and
peered in. There were silver saucepans
and black baking trays and big heavy
frying pans, but she couldn't see a jelly
mould with long ears and a twitchy nose
anywhere.

"Keep looking," Grandma said, filling
the kettle at the sink.

As Lily started taking out the clangy,
clattery pots and pans, the kettle began to
boil. It made a whispery rustling sound

at first, like someone telling a secret, and then, as the water heated up, the noise became a rushing, roaring sound, like a tumbling waterfall.

There were all sorts of familiar things in Grandma's cupboard. There was a dish with a blue lid that Grandma always served roast potatoes in. There were the red plastic plates which she and Archie had used for picnics in the garden, and sometimes at the beach. And there was the big white sieve that Grandpa used when he was washing fresh fruit and vegetables from the garden. But where was the jelly mould?

"Are you sure it's in here?" Lily asked, peering into the dark corners of the cupboard.

"Definitely," Grandma replied. "Keep looking," she said again.

Lily was practically right inside the cupboard before she saw something tucked away, right in the furthest, most shadowy corner. Aha! What was that?

Lily picked up her discovery and crawled backwards out of the cupboard so that she could look at it. It was a glass jelly mould in the shape of a rabbit. "Oh! Long ears and a twitchy tail. . ." Lily laughed. "And Archie really loves rabbits. They are his favourite animals in the world. Well, apart from you, Hector, of course."

Once she'd put everything else back in the cupboard, Lily picked up the jelly mould and did some bouncy bunny hops all the way over to Grandma. "What do we do next?" she asked, wiggling her nose like a real rabbit.

Grandma checked the recipe. "Strawberries! Hmmm. I wonder if the

corner shop is still open?"

Lily grinned. "We don't need to go to the *shop*, Grandma," she said. "Grandpa said that the ones in the garden are ready to eat! Shall I ask him if we can have some?"

"What a good idea," Grandma said. "Yes, please, Lily."

Lily put the jelly mould on the table, then bunny-hopped out of the back door with Hector padding alongside her. She reached over and scratched him behind his soft furry ears, just where he liked it best. "I'm a rabbit now, not a mouse," she told him as he purred. "Catch me if you can!"

And with that she hopped down the lawn, imagining her long fluffy ears flicked up on her head. Bounce, bounce, bounce she jumped towards Grandpa.

Grandpa was kneeling by the strawberry plants, humming to himself as he picked

one ripe strawberry after another and
put them in a bowl. Lily's nose twitched
in a rabbity way. They smelled totally
yummalicious!

"Boing, boing, BOING!" she cried,
with one last enormous bounce that took
her all the way to Grandpa.

Grandpa was so surprised he jumped, and the strawberries went flying up into the air. Lily and Grandpa both burst out laughing as they dived to catch the falling fruit. Even Hector looked as if he was smiling!

"Where did you spring from, Lilybee?" Grandpa chuckled.

"I just came to see if we could have some strawberries," Lily said. "Me and Grandma are making Get-Better Jelly for Archie."

"Get-Better Jelly, hmmmm, that sounds lovely," Grandpa smiled. "Well, in that case, you may certainly have some," he continued. "Especially if you help me pick the last few."

Lily helped Grandpa pick the ripe red strawberries from the strawberry plants. She loved the way the glossy fruit hung from the long thin shoots like beautiful dangly earrings.

As she knelt next to Grandpa in the warm garden, she saw the blue butterfly flit past once more, a scarlet ladybird scrambling over the leaves of a nearby plant and a fat pink worm disappearing into the earth. Archie would be sorry he'd missed seeing that, she thought. He was very keen on worms and creepy crawlies!

"That's probably enough," Grandpa said after a while. "Let's take this lot into the kitchen and wash them. But first, we need to do something very, very important."

"What's that?" Lily asked.

"We need to test them and make sure they're OK," Grandpa said. And before Lily could say another word, he'd popped a strawberry into his mouth.

Lily grinned and took a bite out of a fat strawberry too. The sweet, warm fruit tasted like summer. "Delicious," she declared. "This is definitely going to be the best Get–Better Jelly *ever*!"

4

Let's Get Cooking!

Once she had skipped back inside with the strawberries, Lily carefully washed them in the white sieve, splashing cold water all over them. They were as glossy and shiny as jewels when she'd finished – the best kind of treasure!

Lily then she read out the first line of the recipe. "Ask a grown-up to help you chop the tops off the strawberries, then cut them in half," she said.

"OK," said Grandma, getting out a

knife and a small wooden chopping board. She tipped her head on one side and gave Lily a thoughtful look, then nodded. "I'd better do the chopping," she said. "We don't want any fingers in the jelly! Why don't you line them up for me, Lily?"

"OK." Lily smiled. She arranged the plump strawberries on the board, then watched as Grandma took them one by one and cut off their leafy tops.

"It looks like you're taking their hats off," Lily giggled.

Chop, chop, chop went the knife as Grandma removed the strawberry hats and quickly cut the strawberries in half.

Lily peered at the recipe. "Next it says we have to put the strawberry pieces in the jelly mould," she read. "Can I do that, Grandma?"

"Of course," Grandma said, putting the knife and chopping board safely in the sink.

Lily enjoyed arranging the strawberry pieces in the mould. She made sure there were two pieces right where the rabbit's eyes would be, and lined up some little bits to fit perfectly in the rabbit's ears. Her fingers turned pink from strawberry juice and she couldn't resist licking them afterwards. Mmmm!

"That looks lovely," Grandma smiled. "Now we need to break the jelly into cubes. We just need two of the packets for now; we'll do something else with the other packet later."

"OK," Lily said. Grandma passed her the block of jelly and she began pulling the cubes apart and dropping them into a bowl. The red jelly was stretchy and sticky between her fingers, and sparkled in the bowl as she plopped each cube in.

Grandma read the next instruction. "Dissolve the jelly cubes in hot water," she said. "Do you know what dissolve means?"

Lily shook her head.

"It means we have to make the jelly cubes melt into a liquid," Grandma explained. "That's why the water has to be hot. So how much water do we need, Lily?"

Lily checked the recipe. "One hundred and fifty millilitres," she read.

Grandma put a see-through measuring jug on the table, then picked up the kettle. "It's boiling water so we have to take care," she said. "I'll pour, you tell me when to stop."

Lily crouched down in front of the jug and watched as Grandma carefully tipped hot water into it. The steaming water passed the mark for fifty millilitres, then one hundred, then. . . "Stop!" Lily cried, just in time.

"Perfect," Grandma said, handing Lily a wooden spoon. "If I pour the water on to the jelly cubes, can you stir it round, please? Nice and slowly, though, because the water's very hot and I don't want you to splash yourself with it."

Lily watched Grandma pour the hot water into the bowl, then stirred the mixture very carefully. Straight away the jelly cubes stopped having such square sides and began softening around the edges. Soon they were jelly blobs, and the water turned pinky-red. But even though Lily stirred and stirred, the blobs wouldn't dissolve any more.

"Grandma," she said, "it's not working."

"Oh, that's all right," said Grandma, as she came over to have a look. "The water must have cooled down. We'll just warm it back up," she said as she poured the jelly water mix into a saucepan and placed on the hob.

Lily kept stirring and soon the water was scarlet and steaming and a delicious strawberry smell filled the kitchen. It looked just like a magic potion, Lily thought. Now the water was scarlet and steaming and a delicious strawberry smell filled the kitchen. It looked just like a magic potion, Lily thought.

"Wonderful!" Grandma exclaimed. "And not a single drop spilled. Well done, Lily. Now for the lemonade. There's a new bottle in the Yummy Cupboard. Could you get it for me, please?"

"OK," Lily said, going to find it. The

bottle of lemonade was big and heavy, and she had to use both arms to carry it to the table. Then, when Grandma took the lid off the bottle, there was a *psshhht!* noise and lots of tiny bubbles rushed up the bottleneck. The sound made Hector's ears swivel in surprise, and Lily giggled at his startled expression.

"Can you check the amount while I pour?" Grandma asked.

Lily glanced at the recipe. "We need four hundred and twenty millilitres this time." She crouched down again as Grandma poured the lemonade into the jug, and watched as the level of the fizzing, bubbling liquid rose up and up. She could hear the tiny bubbles popping on the surface. "Stop!" she cried when the jug was nearly full.

Lily tipped the lemonade into the bowl of jelly water and stirred. Now the magic

potion looked paler pink and smelled
even sweeter.

"Perfect," Grandma declared. "The
mixture can go into the rabbit mould
now, and then the whole thing can go
into the fridge to set."

Once the jelly and lemonade potion
was in the mould, with the strawberries

bobbing in it like tiny boats, Lily carefully slid the rabbit into an empty space in the fridge. "I hope it doesn't take too long to set," Lily said, peering at it impatiently. "I can't wait to try it!"

5

Grandma's Surprise

Grandma asked Lily to start breaking up the leftover packet of jelly into cubes while she went to check on Archie. "Fast asleep and snoring," she said when she came back. "Which means we can make more jelly!"

"Are we making another rabbit, Grandma?" Lily asked, tearing the last two red cubes apart. They wobbled as she dropped them into the bowl.

"Not this time," Grandma said, bending

down to get something out of the cupboard. She set a large shallow tray on the table. "We're going to put the jelly mixture in here instead."

"Oh," said Lily. She was a tiny bit disappointed. Ordinary jelly sounded rather boring after the special Get-Better Jelly they'd made in the rabbit mould.

"Don't worry," Grandma said, seeing Lily's expression. "I've got big plans for this jelly. We'll do something fun with it a bit later."

"What sort of thing?" Lily wanted to know.

Grandma tapped her nose mysteriously. "It's a surprise," she replied. "Wait and see!"

This time, they mixed up the jelly the ordinary way, with hot and cold water, and no strawberries or lemonade. "It seems less sloshy than the last mixture," Lily commented as she stirred.

"That's because we've put less water in it this time," Grandma said. "This is one of my old recipes. Your mum used to make this kind of jelly with me when she was a little girl, you know."

"Did she?" Lily loved the idea of her mum baking with Grandma when she was little.

"Oh yes," Grandma said. "She would beg me to let her make jelly like this because. . . Well, you'll see. She always had lots of fun with it."

Lily was starting to feel more excited about the second jelly recipe. If her mum had loved it, she was certain she would too. And Grandma's surprises always turned out to be wonderful!

By now, the last blobs of jelly had dissolved, so Lily poured the mixture into the tray. Then, still wondering what Grandma was going to do to make this jelly exciting, she slid the tray of runny red mixture into the fridge to set.

Just at that moment, they heard a shout from the living room. "Where's everyone *gone*? I'm *bored*!" Then came some coughing followed by a wail. "And I still feel poorly!"

Lily carefully touched the tip of her finger into the jelly in the rabbit mould, but it was still gooey and wet. It hadn't set yet.

"Oh no, the Get-Better Jelly isn't ready," she said. "How are we going to make Archie feel better without it?"

Grandma ruffled her hair. "We'll just have to keep him entertained while we wait for the Get-Better Jelly to set," she said. "See if you can think of something while I clean up in here."

Lily washed her hands and went into the living room, thinking hard. She was determined to cheer up her poorly little brother . . . but how?

6

A Cheering-Up Challenge

"Hi, Archie," Lily said as she went into the living room. "How are you feeling?"

The blanket was twisted around Archie's legs and he looked hot and bad-tempered as she went over to the sofa. "Not very well," he grumbled. "Everything hurts and I'm fed up."

"I know what will cheer you up," Lily said as an idea popped into her head. "Silly Lily's Funny Faces!"

Lily knew her funny faces always made

Archie laugh. She
squished her cheeks
together with both
hands, went cross-
eyed and poked
her tongue out.

Archie smiled.

Lily pushed her
nose up like a pig's,
stuck her front teeth out like a rabbit's
and stretched up her eyebrows as high as
they'd go.

Archie giggled.

Lily pulled her eyes downwards, put
a thumb on the end of her nose and
waggled her fingers, then stuck her
tongue out of the side of her mouth and
made a noise like a seal honking. To top
it off, she did a silly dance, kicking her
feet up behind her.

Archie burst out laughing . . . and Lily smiled in delight. She'd done it. She'd cheered up her brother!

But seconds later, Archie's laugh turned into a wheezy cough. He coughed and coughed until his face turned bright red and his eyes watered. Lily felt really bad. Oh no. She hadn't meant *that* to happen!

"Are you OK? Do you want some water?" she asked, rushing over.

Archie shook his head and flopped back against the sofa. All his smiles and giggles were gone.

"Sorry," Lily said. Maybe she'd been *too* funny. She'd have to think of a different way to cheer him up. "I know," she said, as a new idea came to her. "I'll show you some of the things we were doing in drama today. We had to cross the room in different ways. We took giant steps. . ."

She showed him, stretching her legs right out in enormous strides.

"We waddled like ducks. . ."

She stuck her bottom out and wiggled imaginary tail feathers while flapping her wings. Archie smiled again. "I like ducks," he croaked.

"We fluttered like fairies. . ."

Lily danced lightly across the room, flapping her arms as if they were shimmering fairy wings.

"And we stomped like dinosaurs."

Archie sat bolt upright immediately as Lily began stomping and stamping and roaring like a dinosaur. "I want to be a dinosaur too," he said, scrambling eagerly off the sofa.

Archie tried to roar . . . but his voice was too croaky.

Then he tried to stomp . . . but his legs were too shaky. He fell over on his bottom and started to cry. "My head hurts," he sobbed.

Lily hurried over to him. "Oh Archie, let me help you," she said. Poor Archie felt very hot and heavy as Lily helped him clamber back on to the sofa. The Get-Better Jelly could not be ready soon enough, Lily thought to herself.

After she'd made Archie comfortable with a nice cool cushion under his head and the blanket tucked cosily around his legs, Lily had another idea. Of course! "How about some cartoons?" she asked, turning on the television. Archie loved cartoons, almost as much as dinosaurs, football and rabbits.

Archie smiled as Lily turned on the TV and a cartoon cat and dog appeared on screen. Lily knew this show was one of his favourites, and sat down at the other end of the sofa to watch it with him. Phew – at last. She'd finally found something which would cheer Archie up, and which didn't make him cough or fall over. Mission accomplished!

Archie settled down contentedly with his thumb in his mouth. Lily was feeling so worn out herself that she curled up at the other end of the sofa and pulled the blanket over her legs too.

Lily snuggled down opposite Archie and pulled over a cushion to use as a pillow. It was quite nice to be all curled up on the sofa with her little brother. Archie gave a huge yawn, and it made Lily yawn too. She started to watch the TV programme, but after a minute she felt her eyes closing. She was so warm and cosy that she couldn't help falling fast asleep!

The next thing Lily knew, Grandma was gently waking her up. "Mum will be here soon," Grandma said. "But before then, I think our special you-know-what might be ready. Shall we see?"

Lily blinked and rubbed her eyes. It took her a second to realize what Grandma was talking about, but then she jumped to her feet in excitement. The Get-Better Jelly was done!

Jelly on a Plate

Lily glanced over at Archie, who was still curled up watching the television. "You snored," he giggled.

Lily laughed. Archie must be a bit better if he was being cheeky! "I'll bring you some of your surprise as soon as I can," she told him, then followed Grandma into the kitchen.

Grandma filled the sink with some warm water and Lily frowned.

"What do we need that for?" she asked,

puzzled. "Are we going to give the rabbit a bath?"

Grandma chuckled. "Well, sort of," she said. "If you get the jelly mould out of the fridge and bring it over here, I'll tell you what to do next."

Lily opened the fridge door and slid the cold rabbit mould out. She couldn't resist giving the top of the jelly a gentle prod. Boing! The jelly was now smooth and perfectly set, and her finger bounced back as if it were on a springy trampoline.

"If we dip the mould into the warm water, it will help the jelly come out nice and smoothly," Grandma told Lily as she took the jelly to the sink. "So let's lower it in for a few seconds, but make sure you don't let the water come over the edge of the mould. We don't want a soggy rabbit!"

The mould was dripping wet when Lily took it out of the water again and she gave it a little shake, sending droplets splashing back into the sink like rain. Hector was watching from the window sill and looked very surprised at the indoor shower.

"Now for a plate to put the jelly on," Grandma said, bustling over to the dresser.

"Can we have a *green* plate, Grandma?" Lily asked. "Then it'll look like the rabbit's sitting on some grass."

"Good thinking," Grandma said, her eyes twinkling as she found a special grass-green plate. "I hope it doesn't start nibbling holes in my china, though!"

Together Lily and Grandma tipped the mould over so that it sat on the green plate. Then they tapped the mould a few times with the end of a wooden spoon.

"Out you come, little rabbit," Grandma said, shaking the mould gently.

Lily held her breath and slowly lifted the mould . . . but the jelly hadn't budged. "Nothing's happening!" she cried.

No sooner had she said the words, though, when there was a great squishy squelch, and out plopped the rabbit on to the plate with a shiver and a shudder.

Grandma carefully lifted the mould away and Lily laughed in delight at the wibbly-wobbly red jelly rabbit that sat in front of her, with strawberry eyes and ears and strawberries dotted over his back. "Hurray!" she cheered. "He's lovely!"

"What's lovely?" came a little voice in the doorway.

Lily and Grandma both looked round to see Archie standing there, his thumb in his mouth, with the blanket trailing on the floor behind him.

"Hello, poppet," Grandma said, going over to hug him. "Come and see what your clever big sister has been doing."

"We've made Get-Better Jelly for you," Lily said, pointing at the jelly rabbit. "Would you like to try some? It's got real strawberries in!"

Archie nodded, a big smile on his face. "I like jelly," he said. "And I like strawberries. And I really *really* like rabbits."

Grandma laughed. "That's lucky," she said. "Sit down at the table, Archie, and I'll give you each a bowlful." She winked. "There might even be some extra strawberries for two very good children."

Just at that moment, the back door opened and Grandpa came in, wiping his feet on the mat. "Ooh, jelly!" he exclaimed, seeing the rabbit. "Is there any left for a very good grandpa too?"

Grandma smiled. "I think there might be," she said. "But only very good grandpas who wash their hands first!"

Archie and Lily giggled as Grandpa hurried to the sink and immediately started scrubbing his fingers. "How are you feeling there, Archie?" he asked. "Still looking a bit pink in the cheeks, I see."

"He's still a bit hot," Grandma agreed, putting a hand on Archie's forehead. "But luckily, Lily has made the perfect thing for him."

"It's Get-Better Jelly, Grandpa," Lily explained proudly.

Grandpa dried his hands on the tea towel and sat down next to her. "Splendid," he said. "Just what every patient needs!"

Grandma got out four bowls, four little spoons and one big serving spoon. She plunged the spoon into the rabbit, which made another lovely squelchy noise, and carefully cut one jelly ear for Lily and the wriggly rabbit tail for Archie. "There you go," she said, passing them their bowls.

Lily popped a spoonful of the springy, smooth Get-Better Jelly into her mouth. "Mmmm! It is fizzy!" she said, feeling the bubbles popping on her tongue. "And the strawberries are so lovely and cold."

"It's all soft and slidey on my sore throat," Archie said, looking happier than he'd done all afternoon. "Yum, yum."

"Well, I'm glad you like it," Grandma said, spooning some jelly into bowls for her and Grandpa too. "And I'm sure the Get–Better magic will start working very soon!"

8

Jolly Jelly

For a few moments there were no sounds apart from the scraping of spoons against bowls and the slurping of jelly. Lily put her last spoonful into her mouth and enjoyed the way its cool sweetness melted on her tongue. Yum! "Jelly on a plate, jelly on a plate," she sang, jumping up from her chair. "Wibble-wobble, wibble-wobble, jelly on a plate." As she sang the words, she wibble-wobbled from side to side, just like the wobbly strawberry jelly.

Hector wound himself around Lily's legs, nearly tripping her up, and Archie giggled.

"Whoa!" Lily laughed, reaching down to stroke Hector. "Are you being a wibbly-wobbly cat?" Then she grinned at Archie. "I definitely feel good after my Get-Better Jelly," she said. "How about you?"

Archie smiled. "I feel a bit better," he said.

Grandma put a hand on Archie's forehead to check the temperature. "You *do* seem cooler, Archie," she said. "The jelly magic must have worked!" She glanced up at the kitchen clock and smiled. "And that's lucky, because we've just got time to have some fun with the second batch of jelly."

"Oh yes!" Lily said. She'd almost

forgotten about the jelly in the tray. What was Grandma's surprise going to be?

Grandpa cleared their bowls away and Grandma brought the tray of jelly over to the table. "I'll do my finger-trampoline test on it," Lily announced. "Watch this, Archie."

She jumped a finger gently on to the flat, smooth jelly. *Boing!* went her finger, bouncing back. "Yes, it's definitely set," Lily said with a grin.

"Can I try?" Archie said at once.

"Are your fingers clean?" Grandma asked. "OK, then. One little bounce!"

Boing! went Archie's finger,

and he gave a big chuckle as the jelly sprang back under his touch. "Jelly is the best," he said.

"It's not as bouncy as the rabbit jelly," Lily realized, turning to Grandma anxiously. "Maybe we should have put some more water in it?"

"Don't worry," Grandma said mysteriously. "We need it to be a bit firmer than normal jelly. You'll see why in a minute," she added, rummaging in a cupboard. Lily watched impatiently as Grandma brought out a biscuit tin. What were they going to do?

"Here we go," Grandma said, putting the tin on the table. Lily and Archie leaned closer as she pulled off the lid. Inside were lots of different kinds of biscuit cutters that she normally used to make fun-shaped cookies.

"Because this jelly's firmer, we can use these to cut it into jelly shapes, like big versions of the jelly sweets you buy in the shops," Grandma explained. "We can have jelly stars, jelly hearts, jelly cats . . . and even. . ." She held one of the biscuit cutters up in the air and Archie squealed with delight.

"Jelly dinosaurs!" Lily laughed.

"Jelly *dinosaurs*," Archie echoed happily with the biggest smile he'd had all day.

Grandma passed him the cutter and he squidged it straight into the jelly. Then, with Grandma's help, he lifted out the jelly dinosaur he'd cut. "Wow!" he gasped. "Look at him!"

Grandpa turned around from where he was washing up and pretended to gasp in fear at the sight of a real, red dinosaur in the kitchen. "I hope it's not a fierce one," he said, looking scared.

"Oh, he's *very* fierce," Archie said, as Grandma helped him poke the red wobbly dinosaur out of the cutter and on to a plate. "But don't worry, Grandpa. I won't let him get you." While everyone watched, Archie picked the dinosaur up and bit his head off in one mouthful.

"Phew," Grandpa said, putting a hand on his heart. "I was getting worried, then. Thanks for saving me, Archie."

Archie grinned. "Wait till I tell Mum I've eaten a *dinosaur*!" he chuckled with his mouth full.

Lily and Grandma exchanged a smile. Archie was *definitely* feeling better now. He cut out three more dinosaurs, making happy roaring sounds, then made the dinosaurs have a sticky, messy fight with each other on the plate. Splodges of jelly went everywhere, but Grandma didn't seem to mind.

Lily was busy cutting out jelly hearts

and stars. "They're almost too pretty to eat," she said, licking her lips as she arranged them on a plate. But the jelly smelled so yummy and fruity, she couldn't resist popping a star into her mouth. "Mmmm," she said happily. This jelly was a bit chewier than the Get-Better Jelly, and it wasn't fizzy, but it still tasted just as delicious.

Grandma cut out a jelly cat and managed to stand him up on a plate so that Hector could see him. Hector opened his green

eyes very wide and gave a loud meow
when he saw the gleaming red jelly cat.

When the jelly had all been cut and
everyone had finished eating, Lily asked
Grandma if she could get down the

special recipe box from where it was kept up on the dresser. The box was covered in pretty flowery paper, and was the perfect place to store all the recipes that came from the magic jar.

"There," said Lily, writing "Get-Better Jelly" in her neatest handwriting on the top of the recipe and carefully tucking it inside.

"And next time anyone feels ill, we know just what to do."

"Make more Get-Better Jelly!" Archie and Grandma chorused, smiling.

Grandpa clutched his throat. "You know, I think I'm coming down with something," he said, with a loud pretend cough. "Maybe we should make some more Get-Better Jelly just in case. . ."

Everyone laughed. "Poor Grandpa," Lily said, putting her arms around him. "I'll give you a Get-Better cuddle instead."

As Grandpa hugged her and told he was feeling better already, Lily caught sight of Grandma's magic jar, back up on the dresser. The sun sparkled through the window again, and Lily felt her heart thump as the jar seemed to twinkle and gleam with

magic. She couldn't wait to see
which recipe it gave them next!

Look out for more

Bake a Wish

books

Bake a Wish

Feel Good Fairy Cakes

Includes FANTASTIC cut-out-and-keep recipe card!

Lorna Honeywell

Bake a Wish

Can-Do Crispies

Includes FANTASTIC cut-out-and-keep recipe card!

Lorna Honeywell

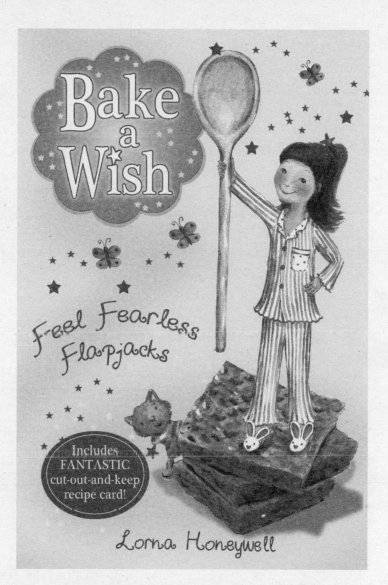

Look out for

Mend-it
Muffins

and

Friendship
Fudge

Coming soon!

Bake
a
Wish

For more baking
fun and extra
recipes visit

www.scholastic.co.uk/zone